Katie's

A Ghost and the Disappearing Castle

By

Jasmine Appleton

Copyright © Jasmine Appleton 2017

Written with British spelling.

Book 5 in the collection of Katie's magic camera.

Chapter One
Girl or Ghost?

Amy looked out from a window positioned high up in this building, the one she was staying in with her school friends, after traveling down from Scotland to Nottingham in England. The old building with its many dormitories went back centuries and Amy thought the place must hold many secrets within its historic walls. Really she was thinking, did Robin Hood ever stand where she stood now?

It was dark behind Amy as her knee touched a damp stone wall, her eyes searching from that window, looking for Jessica, her best friend, who she had left talking with a teacher at the arched entrance doors of this building. What did Mr Woodstock want with her?

Amy didn't hear anyone coming up from behind her, but she felt a furry body brush past her ankles. When she looked down she saw a scruffy black cat with half an ear missing, run from her feet. Amy thought she recognised that cat, but where from? She frowned as she searched her memory.

"Boo," a crackly voice called out, from the shadows, making her jump and spin around, to see no one was there. She shuddered from a chill hanging in the air that carried that voice; was she hearing things? Why did she feel so cold, as if a ghost had floated about and touched her body? Then she remembered that black cat. It looked just like the one she had met in Cordren's den two summers ago, when she was deep inside a castle, hidden in the secret garden of Princess Isabel.

Cordren was a dark, bad witch and Amy's enemy, but still, Amy didn't know why Cordren and her own family disliked each other so much!

Turning back to the window, Amy peered out once again to see that Jessica had moved from the doors and was heading away, across a huge lawn. Where was she going?

Amy had to stand on tiptoe to rub at the dirty pane of glass and see clearer. She looked towards a building holding a museum, a building beyond that lawn, where she and her class would be visiting tomorrow. But why was Jessica going over there now and on her own, at this late time of day? Amy was always full of questions.

From where she stood, Amy had been expecting to see an ancient castle surrounded by tall walls, round turrets and a drawbridge where Prince John, one day to become King John of England would have entered, but no, all she could see was a thirteenth-century gateway and a seventeenth-century building over the far side of that wide lawn. Well, that's the ages the buildings were, according to the school's bus driver. Nottingham Castle was the building Amy had wanted to see, the castle where Prince John was supposed to have stayed when on his journeys from London to the north of England, hundreds of years ago and where Robin Hood fought with both the Sheriff of Nottingham and the Prince.

Amy had seen her father watching many films on their TV, of Robin Hood, the outlaw, who it's said, robbed the rich to give to the poor. But was he just that, an actor in a film, a legend, from a time past by now? Amy's imagination was a wonderful thing to have.

Amy thought her teacher had brought her and her classmates here to learn all about Nottingham's history, including King Richard the Lion Heart, who went abroad to fight in the Crusades, who had left his brother, Prince John behind in England to rule his land as Prince Regent.

Amy gave out a slow, deep sigh, for all she could see were a few old broken down walls with an archway through to the shops hiding just inside the castle's ruins. Well, that's what she thought she could see, but they weren't clear to her eye.

Amy had also been told of the honeycomb caves under the shopping center, caves forged from sandstone worn away by the weather. Places to explore, for very different reasons; Amy was taking more notice of fashion now she was heading towards becoming a teenager and she wanted to go shopping with her friends. And of course, there was the lace making, this city of Nottingham had also been renowned for in the past, but Amy was not going to buy any! Her mum might have if she had been here, but not her!

She had learned of the Nottingham caves from Mr Woodstock in her history lessons; they sounded interesting. Those caves had held prisoners long ago, as well as being storage places. Yes she thought, they could be interesting too but so would shopping and she smiled to herself.

Amy then remembered the cave in Cornwall on her last school trip; she wanted none of that nonsense this trip. Oh no! No missing boys to find and save from swordsmen and dragons this time. But she did fancy some excitement here on this school trip. Any adventure would make her happy. Amy had a different life to her other school friends, well, other than Jess, of course, Amy let Jess join her in her adventures.

Amy now had a vision forming in her head from earlier that day, when their school bus had driven her class through Sherwood Forest, where once kings had taken out their noble friends from the royal court, in hunting parties, the bus driver had also told her class that day. Commoners were not allowed to hunt those areas of land; it was a crime for them to kill the King's deer.

The bus had passed by many trees, some young saplings others old with wrinkled trunks. Suddenly the bus had had to swerve sharply to miss a dark shadowy person dashing across the narrow road between those trees. Whoever it was had disappeared before a white ghostly figure who also faded away.

"Hang on!" The bus driver had shouted at the top of his voice, as he held on tight to his steering wheel, his foot pushing down hard on the brake. The bus had leaned to one side, running along on only its side wheels, finally coming to a standstill before a huge old oak tree. With a jolt and a wobble, the bus stopped just in time before hitting that tree and tipped back onto all its wheels. The youngsters inside the bus had shouted and squealed.

Mr Woodstock and his class had been rocked about in that bus, some girls shrieking as boys and girls fell from their seats to sit in the aisles. Youngsters, like Sam, the trouble-making boy in

7

school who had not been wearing their seat belts, now sat awkwardly on the bus's floor, but luckily no one was hurt.

When the bus swerved, Mr Woodstock had been explaining about and pointing with his finger to an old oak tree, the one that was over eight hundred years old.

After the driver had managed to straighten up his bus, taken a huge breath to calm himself he had driven on at a much slower pace and everyone sat quietly in their seats, not sure of what had caused the driver to hit his brakes so suddenly.

But Amy thought she knew why it had happened. She had seen two shadowy figures sitting in the branches and another one dashing over the road who she knew - Cordren!

*

This old tree had a massive hollow in its trunk and its twisting branches spread out for over a hundred feet. Robin Hood could have met with his merry men under that very tree, or even sat amongst its branches, Amy thought, as she sat glaring out of the bus's window before all that excitement had happened.

But where had the shadowy figures disappeared to? Amy wondered some more.

"If only trees could talk, what a lot they could tell us," Jessica turned to Amy and said.

"If only," Amy replied, before noticing the specks of gold, twinkling, jumping lights flitting amongst the trees. What were those lights? She thought of fairies perhaps and Amy remembered the golden fairy lady, her friend that only Jessica and she knew of, although Thomas had also met her, but now had no memory of that meeting.

There had been no other dark or scary shadows hovering between those tree trunks in the forest, so hopefully, there were no nasty witches hiding, but were there?

Amy had found small witches in trees in her very first adventure when meeting Katie, her mermaid friend, who now kept the magic camera. Amy held that thought in her mind. She had made some strange friends since staying at her Aunt Flora's cottage that first summer holiday. But Amy did so wish for another adventure here, as nothing had happened since the New Year, after her birthday, on the day when she had been given a cube from the golden fairy lady and heard her aunt's words, 'your life will change now you have hold of that cube.' Amy had brought the cube with her on this trip and she looked across to where her bag laid now, under the bunk beds, the cube hidden amongst her clothes. Her aunt had added, those changes would come slowly before she became a teenager next New Year when she would hold so many powers, but that birthday wasn't for another nine months and Amy could hardly wait.

A hand touched Amy on the shoulder; she jumped and forgot what she was thinking about. Jessica had come up behind her.

"What are you looking at?" She asked Amy.

"Oh, nothing," and asked Jessica the question. "What did Mop Head want?" That was the name the youngsters called Mr Woodstock, their history teacher because he was tall and thin like a broom handle with a mop of fair hair on his head.

"Oh, he asked about the project I am writing."

"Oh, I see," said Amy and stepped away from the window as a sudden flash of blinding light shot passed outside. But there was no thunder. Amy turned back to try and look through a swirling white mist which had been left behind, a mist she thought was a flash of white fire, who would send fire? Only one person, Cordren the witch!

"What is it?" Jessica asked her friend, as she could see nothing herself and her friend looked worried.

Amy still peered out of the window, but at what? Jessica really couldn't see anything different.

Amy rubbed at her eyes and pointed with her finger.

"There Jess, look a complete full-size castle."

Jessica couldn't see any completed castle, only ancient parts of a fallen down wall, the lawn and the museum.

"Jess it's a castle, just passed where you walked over that lawn."

"I never walked over there," Jessica snapped back.

"But I saw you." Amy was so very sure in her reply.

Amy felt confused as she studied Jessica's face to see if she was joking, but no, she wasn't.

"Come on, we have to go down for dinner."

Jessica pulled at Amy's sleeve to try and move her from the window and as Amy glanced back the castle had disappeared as the ghostly figure had too. How strange!

*

It had been a long drive down from Scotland and as ever Jessica was hungry.

"But Jess, it was you," Amy said again as she moved from the window.

Jessica was getting tired of Amy going on about this, she wanted to eat.

"I wasn't there," she said and walked off into the corridors, heading towards the main dining hall.

Arriving at the wide open oak doors and walking into a full dining hall, Jessica noticed Thomas.

"Look, over there, there's Tom, look, he's looking at you." Jessica was trying to change the subject and pulled at Amy's sleeve once again as she joked about her silly crush on Thomas.

Amy blushed and looked the other way; she really liked Thomas, but wouldn't let anyone know how she felt. Did Thomas feel the same way about her?

Maybe! Were they too young? Another maybe sat in Amy's mind.

Amy thought perhaps they were but she wanted him as a good friend because he was always fun to be with and could ride a horse really well, after his grandfather's schooling. When Amy's family visited his farm, Amy had ridden horses too.

Actually, Thomas couldn't make Amy out. Whenever he was around her, strange things seemed to happen, which messed with his head and his memory. Thomas shook his head as Amy moved away, dismissing things that made no sense to him, and he went to sit with his friends, Andy and Matt who had also been caught up in last autumn's magical school trip to Cornwall, but they couldn't remember that ancient time either.

The girls sat down on the other side of the hall, well away from the boys and Amy started on Jessica again.

"Why did you go to the museum and why do you keep changing your clothes, Jess?"

That was it; Jessica asked if Amy was seeing things. That wouldn't surprise Jessica; after all, she had been to some strange places with Amy and met some unusual people and animals. Talking animals; she remembered a teddy bear that Amy had cuddled and it later turned into a grizzly bear. That was very strange, but perhaps not as strange as Katie, Amy's mermaid friend, who had legs that grew in place of her tail, when that became dry!

Enjoying dinner Amy kept quiet for a change and with no more questions, she thought for a while about what that girl on the lawn was wearing. She looked like Jessica even though her skin appeared pale, as far as Amy had seen from her window and Jessica always had a lovely tanned skin because her grandparents and father came from a Caribbean island and her mother being Scottish had such pale skin and red hair. But both the girls had black curly hair. So who was that girl, if it wasn't Jessica? Amy was concentrating, thinking, that girl on the lawn wore a brown skirt with a ragged hemline and a dirty white blouse. Jessica sat next to her in blue jeans and a pink jumper. So who was that other girl?

Amy was nudged by Jessica who had finished eating her meat pie and vegetables covered in thick brown gravy, while Amy had hardly started her food.

"Yes? What now? Amy asked.

"I saw a ghost," Jessica answered.

"What? Don't be so silly," Amy said with a grin on her face.

Jessica did look pale, as though she really had seen a ghost, but she said no more and the girls, along with all the other youngsters headed off to bed.

Amy lay looking up at the ceiling from her top bunk bed as Jessica lay underneath her on the lower bed, making wheezing noises as she slept, having said no more about ghosts.

Amy was watching the pretty coloured spots of lights jumping around the dormitory, as though there was one of those balls from a dance hall spinning overhead. But there was no ball. Amy thought perhaps they were magical lights, like the ones she had first seen in her bedroom at Aunt Flora's or those lights in the forest earlier in the day. Amy got to her feet and looked out of that same window once again and sure enough, there was that girl walking over the lawn again. Amy thought, surely she would be cold in the middle of the night wearing those same clothes, after all, it was still only early spring and nights were still chilly. Amy turned to see Jessica was still sleeping and when Amy turned back to look out again the girl had disappeared, but now a castle stood in front of her. Amy rubbed at her eyes yet again and when she took that second look the castle had disappeared. There was a full moon and no fog to hide anything, so where had that castle gone, and the girl on the lawn, where was she? Who was she? It was all very strange.

Amy was tired and went to lie down to sleep; there would be plenty of time tomorrow to look for a disappearing castle and Jessica's ghost. Was that girl crossing the lawn, Jessica's ghost? Amy really should have listened to her friend. After all, this building was old enough to have ghosts and she had felt a coldness when she thought she heard the word, 'boo' behind her. And what about that black

14

cat? Where did he come from, but more to the point where did he go to? Was he Cordren's cat? Was she here?

Once again in Amy's world, she had more questions, than answers.

Chapter Two
Mist hides time

Having enjoyed a dish full of cereal and a milkshake for breakfast, the two girls were off following the rest of their class, to walk over to the museum housed in the seventeenth-century palace which had replaced the old castle. Once there Mr Woodstock gave his class a guide book of the building and told them to make their notes, for the project the whole class was working on. Jessica was exceedingly good at history and was the team leader on the subject and that's what Mr Woodstock had been discussing with her yesterday.

Everyone was to meet with Mr Woodstock in the museum's cafe at one o'clock for lunch. Friends paired up and set about the task of finding information for their part of the project.

While Jessica wrote her notes, Amy was looking out for ghosts!

"Come on, Amy you haven't written anything yet," Jessica pointed out to her.

But Amy was walking slowly along, reading the transcripts placed under each painting depicting castles and people. This first picture was of a wooden castle built in the year after the battle of Hastings in 1066, where King Harold had died from an arrow in his eye it has been said and from there King William the Conqueror, from Normandy, had taken charge of England. It was he who instructed that wooden castles were to be built throughout the land, including the first wooden Tower of London and here in Nottingham, this one had been built high up away from any attackers, above the caves made of sandstone rocks. Close by the river Trent ran and had in its time been useful for transporting cargo to other cities throughout the country although not so much now.

But all these wooden built castles would be replaced over the following years with stone built castles.

The next line of paintings showed those stone castles, one painting having two rose bushes placed in the landscape surrounding the castle. One red rose bush, that of the House of Lancaster and a white rose, that of the House of York, both depicting the Wars of the Roses which broke out often over a few decades. That had been another time in English history when Nottingham castle had once again been used as a military stronghold.

Many years later, after the English Civil war had ended, this castle had been blown up, on the orders of Parliament, causing most of it to be demolished. This was carried out to make sure no other King of England could use the place to muster an army against Parliament ever again. So now only a gateway and some of the ruined walls were left standing and Amy really should be writing all this information down for her part on the school project,

17

but she wasn't. Amy kept on reading and still no notes were taken. She was looking for paintings of Robin Hood and Maid Marion, along with Will Scarlet and Little John, then she might be interested in taking notes. But there were no paintings of these people; was it true then, Robin and his merry men were all just legends?

Amy carried on down the line of paintings, King Richard I and King Charles I who was executed in London because of the English Civil war, were all looking down on Amy. Paintings of noblemen and ladies came towards the end of the art room. A countryman dressed in keeping with the time, proudly holding his longbow, seemed to peer down too at Amy and suddenly winked at her! Amy jumped back in surprise but had she just imagined it? Pictures don't move, do they?

He could have been anyone but Amy liked to think it was Robin Hood, the hero of the films. The information with this painting read, 'singers sang the ballads of a time when the legendary Robin Hood roamed the forest, he who took from the rich and gave to the poor'.

Perhaps there was a man who gave to the poor and perhaps his name was Robin. A Lord Loxley supposedly had lived close by, so just maybe there was a little truth of a man called Robin Hood. Amy liked to think so; she smiled to herself.

Sam came along with his troublesome group of friends. They had been a difficult bunch on the last school trip and often were in school and now he remarked about how all that history stuff had been thrown at them in class.

"What are you looking at, Amy dreamer?" That's what he called her, as he too, like Thomas couldn't make Amy out, not that Thomas was rude to or about Amy as Sam was. But somehow Amy worried both boys.

"Oh, you believe in Robin Hood, don't you?" Sam said with a snigger and laughed as he ran away muttering under his breath, "Amy dreamer."

Jessica came up to Amy. She had heard what Sam had said and felt sorry for her friend.

"Come on Amy, there may have been a man who was rich and gave to the poor, you know."

Amy smiled back at Jessica and thought, no her friend had it wrong, Robin Hood stole from the rich to give to the poor.

It was almost one o'clock and Amy still hadn't written any notes. Jessica was telling her they had to get to the cafe for lunch, reminding Amy that this afternoon they were going to the fields at the edge of Sherwood Forest for an archery lesson. Jessica was quite excited about this even though she had never held a bow or sent an arrow flying anywhere in her life.

But first Amy had to stop and study that last painting, hanging close to the doorway, that of the castle where a lawn area was, where a pale skinned girl with black curly hair, wearing a white blouse

19

above a short brown skirt stood. She looked very much like Jessica and a cleaner version of the girl Amy had seen crossing that very lawn. Also in the background, a forest stood where smoke moved and drifted up between the branches of trees. The smoke was really moving and coming out from the painting, curling down towards Amy's nose and making her cough; now she knew the man in the other painting had winked at her. She leaned in towards this painting to look closer and could just see a tiny black speck in between those trees.

Amy looked harder at the black mark; it was a person sitting in front of a cauldron and she was stirring a spoon in that pot. Suddenly Amy realised it was Cordren the wicked witch wearing her black pointed hat. Amy jumped back in fright, no surely not, this was painted hundreds of years ago, it couldn't possibly be her, but Amy remembered, she had met King Arthur as a boy and Cordren had been there in his time, so of course, she could have been there in that time! Magic was in this place, Amy just knew it! She was beginning to feel a little excited.

Jessica had walked on towards the cafe and was calling back to Amy who had left the paintings only to stop before a glass case to look at an item displayed inside.

"Come on, hurry up."

"Yes, I'm coming," Amy called after her.

But Amy had stopped to admire a piece of ancient lace and worked into that fine cream lace was the original castle from 1067 standing on a mound of caves. To Amy's surprise, a list of names was stitched around its edge. King Henry, King Richard, Prince John, Robin of Loxley and there was another name, Marion, embroidered underneath the castle, was Marion really a person? Had she lived in that castle?

Amy smiled, pulled her phone from her jeans pocket and took a photo.

"No photos," a tall, well-built museum security man dressed in grey shouted out in a loud stern voice as he lifted his cap and waved Amy on through the doorway.

Amy, feeling very pleased with herself, ran quickly from the display room to catch up with Jessica. Amy had a lot to think about over her lunch and seemed very quiet to her friends.

*

Everyone just had time to return to their dormitories after lunch, before setting off to walk to the field.

Back in the dormitories, the two girls studied the photo of the lace and its patterns. It was very pretty but what did it actually tell them, other than the names of the royals from that age? And the caves showed a tiny scroll on a shelf.

Amy jumped at a sound made by a bird which had flown into the window and had hit it hard.

21

"Oh, poor thing," she said, "it must be winded" and Amy opened the window to see the bird had dropped down onto the lawn below. This bird was like no other the girls had ever seen before; it was covered in golden feathers which shone like the light of the sun. Amy watched as it flapped its tiny wings in distress, leaving a heap of golden feathers close by its side on the grass.

"Come on Jess, let's go down."

Amy ran off, she wanted to think the golden fairy lady had sent the bird. Jessica followed Amy. Once both girls arrived close to the bird it sang and hopped about their feet, every so often it stopped to peck at the pile of feathers it had made. Suddenly the bird was squawking and fluttering up above their heads, a black cat had sprung from nowhere to pounce at that bird, which unbeknown to the girls had earlier escaped that very same cat's jaws.

"There's that cat again," Amy said as she turned to see feathers floating around in the air.

"Shoo." Jessica cried while chasing the cat away.

Amy jumped around catching at the feathers to fill her pockets. Jessica returned to Amy's side as the cat dashed off into the distance and now she helped Amy catch more feathers to place in her own pockets. Amy sat on the grass fingering the soft golden feathers while deep in thought. She was getting impatient, she wanted answers, and she needed them now! What was going on in this city of Nottingham?

"What are we going to do with all these feathers?" Jessica asked.

"I'm not sure, Amy replied but I think they were sent to us for a reason so we had better keep them. Come on we have to catch up with the others."

Both girls ran to join their class.

Chapter Three
The Forest

Lining up, in rows of six, Amy's class were taught how to hold a longbow and let an arrow go. Many arrows fell only feet away from the person with the bow. When it came to Thomas's turn, Amy suddenly stepped forward and pushed him sideways, so he couldn't shoot at the girl standing in front of the round target way off in the field.

"What are you doing?" Thomas shouted angrily at Amy. Mr Woodstock shouting at the same time, "get out of the way, Amy," both voices spoke together.

"Didn't you see that girl?" Amy asked.

"What girl?" Thomas said as he threw his arms up in the air in protest.

Thomas thought, 'oh Amy what is your problem; there is no girl out there'.

All his school friends were here standing close to him and laughing as Mop Head looked bewildered now.

Amy knew what she had seen but now felt silly in front of her class and teacher, who was still scolding her, because that arrow could have landed anywhere and have been dangerous to her and anyone of her friends standing around.

Amy walked away, her head down as Sam laughed at her now.

"Boo, come with me you silly girl," she heard whispered words in her ear.

"Who said that?" Amy asked under her breath, half knowing it was Cordren.

Amy felt that same coldness come floating around her again, like the cold she felt once before in the dormitory. She raised her head to look around, but there was no one close by.

Her class had stepped away as Mr Woodstock called Amy and Jessica to come forward; it was their turn to release their arrows. Both girls took aim and let their arrows go flying, at the very same time. They watched in amazement as the sticks with shining arrow heads and feathered tails whizz through the air. Suddenly the girls were losing sight of their arrows as a mist floated about the field and around their bodies.

As the mist cleared, the arrows struck home, but not in the targets of round coloured rings, which they had aimed at. They had set hard in the bark of an enormous tree.

Both girls looked at each other in great surprise. Where had the rest of the class gone? And Mr Woodstock too, where was he?

Amy and Jessica had little time to ask each other before a misty, grey ghostly figure appeared in front of them. A girl of their own age, Amy thought as she stared at her dirty white blouse and ragged hemmed skirt. This was the girl she had seen before, on the

25

lawn and in front of the target Thomas had aimed at.

"Who are you?" Amy asked.

"My name is Marion," she said as she skipped off towards the forest.

"Who?" A wide-eyed Jessica said to Amy.

Jessica was asking, even more, questions of herself in her head. Maid Marion was the love of Robin Hood, or so it had been said. Amy was shaking her head at Jessica; she understood what Jessica was thinking. Marion was also a legend with no proof of her existence when there was a little proof of Lord Loxley, but stranger things had happened in Amy's life, so she could not dismiss her thoughts, that it could be Marion as a child.

There were rustlings in the overhead, hundred foot branches, of this old oak tree with the large hollow in its trunk, the tree which had been pointed out by Mr Woodstock only yesterday as they drove through the forest and where now Amy and Jessica found themselves.

A shadow moved inside that hollow and the leaves of the tree rustled as though unhappy with whoever was hiding inside it. Who, or what, was up there amongst the leaves? Amy thought as she looked up to see boys hanging by the backs of their knees, swinging their arms around and laughing.

The boys jumped down and surrounded Amy and Jessica.

"Who have we here?" A boy said stepping closer and poking Amy in her middle with the end of his longbow.

Jessica moved closer to Amy, almost holding her hand, as another, rather handsome boy rode up on a tall black stallion, a horse which was far too big for its rider, and as he dismounted he went over to talk to Amy.

"Well, Amy, so you have come to find out more about your family history and help restore Marion from her ghostly shadow, back to the girl she should be?"

He seemed to know who Amy was, but how?

"Have I?" Amy asked from a face of startled expression, thinking that was a lot to say on a first meeting.

Jessica nudged Amy in her side.

"What does he mean? Who is he?" She whispered in Amy's ear.

"The Lady said you would come on your quest for information."

But before Amy could say anything, the boy stopped talking to look up into the tree from where a horn was heard blowing. At the very top of the tree, a boy sat with a huge curved horn in his hands. It was made from bone and he held it to his mouth; he was sending out a warning. Both the girls looked around as the boys quickly disappeared back into the many branches of this tree and the boy with the horse remounted and grab at Amy's arm to pull her up, to sit before him, as Jessica shouted:

"What about me?"

Suddenly Jessica was also whisked up, to sit behind this boy, who told her to sit very still and hold on tight around his waist and to be quiet.

The black stallion galloped off into the forest with its three riders aboard.

It wasn't long before a large group of soldiers appeared through the forest, with what looked like a King or a Prince leading the way. This man wore a gold Crown studded with sparkling jewels of red rubies and dark blue sapphires upon his head of shoulder length black hair. Beautiful clothes of a royal blue velvet jacket half covered by his black cloak trimmed with white fur fell over his horse of dapple grey. The rider's wide legs gripped tight to the horse, legs that had been squeezed into brown leather breeches and feet into black boots.

Amy, Jessica, and the boy rider hid amongst the trees of Sherwood Forest, a much denser forest than when the school bus had passed through, which of course it would be as many trees had been felled over the years.

"Quiet, boy," he whispered in the horse's ear as he rubbed at his neck, to calm him. Boy and girls waited and watched.

"Who's that?" Amy asked another question of this boy she sat with, as Jessica gasped from behind and covered her mouth to silence her own words when she heard the answer.

"Prince John," the boy replied. "But he must not see you, Amy, we need you to help Maid Marion and in return, you will find more news of your past family."

"Maid Marion?" Amy spoke in a hushed voice and wondered about her own family. But the boy didn't answer.

The group of soldiers sliced with their swords at the newly grown spring leaves hanging on small twigs while a couple more dismounted and pushed their swords through the old rotting autumn leaves on the ground.

"There is nothing here," one soldier shouted to another before remounting and riding off deeper into the forest with the Prince leading the way. It had been a hunting party, but were they hunting for food or for Robin Hood?

The boys in the trees moved through treetops to Robin's camp. The black stallion set off at a gallop with his three riders but only the boy and horse knew where they were going. Amy and Jessica could do nothing but hang on.

"See you later," Robin shouted back at the boys in the trees.

"Where are we going?" Amy asked but not with any alarm to her voice, because she knew this was another adventure for her to enjoy. And Jessica, well, she was feeling a little scared but trusted Amy, they would be safe.

"My camp." The words came back from the boy as his horse took off deeper into the forest.

Chapter Four
The Camp

Having ridden for a short while the boy reined his horse to a stop. Jessica slipped from the back of the black stallion as the boy jumped from his saddle and turned to help Amy down.

The rest of the boys, who had been in the tree tops, had already arrived at the camp and sat holding their longbows around a fading fire. They were roughly dressed with grubby hands and faces. Jessica stood close by Amy, as the boys sat crossed legged on the forest floor from where rope ladders rose up the sides of tree trunks. Jessica looked across and her eyes followed one ladder which disappeared into those treetops, where she thought she could just see a wooden tree house linked loosely by swinging rope ladders between each tree.

Amy moved her eyes from boy to boy, who was going to speak first?

"Robin, what are you going to do with these two girls?" A voice came from the back of the group of boys.

Amy turned to see a boy wearing a red jacket hanging on by one arm from one of those ladders. There didn't seem to be any other girls around. Why was that? Amy wondered.

"I'm not sure, Will," Robin said. "Perhaps the Lady knows as she was the one who told us two strange girls would arrive."

Jessica whispered in Amy's ear.

"Did you hear his name? Robin," she said.

Before Amy could answer, Jessica added, "but who's, the Lady?"

Amy wanted to know, as much as Jessica did, they would only have a short time to wait, to have their answers.

A breeze blew gently through the trees and with it came a golden line of dust to float in the air making the leaves rustle from its touch and all the time the line became thicker as it twisted and weaved amongst those leaves. The glittering dust was changing shape, to form that of a lady with wings. It was The Golden Fairy Lady who had arrived to float and hover in front of them, her transparent wings fluttering with the breeze.

"Wow," the word was heard by everyone. Jessica's favourite word had been spoken once again.

"Where did she come from?" Jessica asked Amy, quickly, as Robin stood to greet the fairy.

With a slight bow of his head, Robin took her hand to kiss and said:

"Welcome, My Lady."

The rest of the boys stood to greet her too.

"I see Amy and Jessica have arrived and Katie?" she asked, "has she arrived?"

"No, My Lady, we have to go to the lake to find her."

Amy smiled the biggest smile anyone could smile. She was in another one of her adventures for sure and with her best three friends, Jess, the golden fairy lady and soon Katie with the magic camera would be joining them and of course, there was Robin Hood standing in front of her with his merry men, although they were still only boys.

It was all so exciting, she was on an adventure with her best friends.

But Amy must never tell those boys what the future held for them. Because that would change history and like the boy Arthur, who would be King or legend one day, Robin would have to be treated the same. Amy and Jessica had had to keep quiet once before and would again.

"Where is the lake?"

"Not far from here," Robin answered the fairy.

Amy couldn't understand how Katie would get from Cornwall to Nottingham but then she often couldn't work out how these magical things happened in her life, forgetting the huge river that ran through Nottingham and out to the sea where Katie could have been swimming.

Before Amy could ask any more questions, Robin was talking again.

"Come, I have horses for you both."

From the bushes, a boy walked two horses forward, one a palomino and the other pure white.

"Our horses," Jessica said in great surprise.

She could not understand how they were here either, from Aunt Flora's field in Cornwall and from the future! But she should have known better, after all, this is what happened when she was out with Amy. Wonderful, magical, fantasy moments, all to be enjoyed and Jessica gave out a little giggle of pleasure.

"Thank you, Will Scarlet," Robin said as both girls walked up to the two beautiful horses, stroked their long, elegant necks and whispered in their ears, saying how pleased they were to see them. The horses neighed and shook their heads from side to side, making their manes float in the air. They were also pleased to see the girls.

But wait, a very tall, well-built boy followed with another horse, a bay colour, with black socks, or so it appeared to Amy as she noticed a white blaze down the front of his head. Robin jumped onto this horse, thanked John and held the black stallion's reins, to lead him off through the forest. The girls were expected just to follow and Amy knew then, that black stallion belonged to Katie.

"Come on Jess," Amy shouted at Jessica, who had already mounted her horse, Star, and Amy sat on Pal, two horses both named by Jessica last year. They followed Robin at a trot. Amy was thinking, 'John? Was that Little John? And Will Scarlet, two more names from her dad's films, she remembered.

34

Now, John Little was a man, who was supposed to have lived in these parts and didn't Mr Woodstock say they passed his grave in some churchyard when they drove through a little village when on the school bus?

It wasn't long before a lake came into view. Slowing the horses, Robin and the girls came up to the edge of the lake, where they saw Thomas was sitting.

"What are you doing here?" Amy called over, so shocked to see him and also feeling rather worried as to what Thomas would ask her.

"Don't ask me, one minute I was in a field with a longbow in my hand watching you two girls trying to hit a target and then the next thing a thick fog had rolled over me, and here I am! Who's that?" Thomas asked as he stood up and Amy dismounted her horse.

"Oh, just some boy we met in the forest," Amy said.

She wasn't going to use his name or tell Thomas in what year, they actually were.

There was no time for Thomas to ask Amy any more questions, as she had run off towards a girl with long red curly hair falling down to her waist. Dripping with water Katie smiled at Amy from the lakeside.

"Hello," Amy called as she dashed forward to sit beside Katie. Amy started as she always did, firing question after question at Katie.

35

"Why are we here? How did you swim here? What do we have to do now we are here?" On and on Amy went.

"I can see you haven't changed." Katie laughingly said as she dried her tail in the sun, her legs quickly forming. "You still want to know everything and all at once. Now my turn; is Jess still sorting out puzzles?"

Katie knew from previous adventures, that's what both girls did! Asked questions and sorted out puzzles.

Robin stepped in to talk with Katie as the fairy lady hovered just above the ground, fluttering her wings to help dry Katie's tail.

Thomas looked on, scratching at his head, unsure of a lady with wings and a girl with a mermaid tail.

"You have to go to the caves under the castle," the golden fairy started to explain to Amy and Jessica.

"Why?" Amy asked with a smile and a chuckle, she knew she was asking another question.

"Hidden in there are ancient scrolls depicting the history of the world and many families," the golden fairy told them.

Robin knew getting into those caves wouldn't be easy. He knew there were guards and then the ghost of a girl named Marion who walked from the caves across the grass in the center of the castle; she might scare them. Plus Prince John had his lookouts in the castle too. The people of Robin's village had tried to enter those caves many times before and some had been captured and held there as prisoners while some were never seen again.

"I see you have your camera and the flash bulb for time travel," Amy quietly said to Katie, making sure no one else would hear of its magic.

This flashgun was really just a bulb surrounded by a silver dish that clipped to the top of the magic camera which of course changed everything. The bulb had been found on Imagination Island. Well, that's what Amy thought to have happened, only that was in her dream when she fell and bumped her head at the school Halloween dance and knocked herself out. But if it had only been a dream how did Katie have the flash bulb in her hand? Amy was troubled by her memory of that time, as was Thomas. It was still a blurred and a muddled vision in both their minds, more so with Amy, for she could remember more clearly than Thomas. After all, she knew more than Thomas from her other adventures with Katie.

"Yes, I have the flash bulb," Katie replied to Amy bringing her back from her thoughts.

"And if I focus on you and Jess, you can both go forward or back in time," Katie added.

The golden fairy floated closer to the three girls.

"When a new day starts, you must go to the shops above the caves."

"Oh good," Jessica said quickly. She wanted a new pair of jeans, shopping sounded good to her.

"Why?" Amy asked the golden fairy, who carried on with her instructions.

"Go to the department store, take the lift down to the caves and find the one which is of a much darker sandstone, where there will be a clue on the wall behind the arch. Take Jess to untangle the puzzle. In your time there will be no soldiers and you can walk around freely as tourists."

With that, all said, it was Katie who now aimed her camera at the girls and clicked a button on its side. A bright flash blinded everyone for a moment before the two girls were back, standing close to their beds, startled as to what had happened, time traveling, really? Jessica thought!

Fantastic things always happened to Jessica when Katie was with Amy and she found herself smiling just thinking about it.

The two girls were exhausted and said no more to each other before they were soon asleep, and back in their own time!

Chapter Five
Shopping

Amy was up early that next morning and pulling at Jessica, who still slept in the lower bunk bed.

"Come on, get up." Amy was shaking her friend.

Jessica stirred and pulled her duvet up and over her head.

"Go away, I have had a very strange dream."

"No, you haven't Jess. Come on, we have to get to the shops before the crowds."

Amy said no more in case she was overheard by her other school friends across the room. Jessica peeped out from under her duvet, knowing now that it wasn't a dream; she had been with Amy in one of her adventures.

The girls were soon entering the dining hall and eating breakfast while looking around for Thomas, who was nowhere to be seen.

"Is Tom up yet?" Jessica asked Andy.

"No one has seen him since yesterday, in the field, when that fog came rolling down. Mop Head is very worried."

"He'll turn up," Jessica said adding, "don't call Mr Woodstock that name." She remembered the teacher's name had come about years before, but she didn't like it.

"Amy, Tom's missing."

39

"What?" Amy sounded surprised as she turned and whispered to Jessica, "he must still be at the lake with Robin and Katie."

Now the girls knew they had to get back to that time in history, to rescue Thomas if nothing else. But first, they must find the clue for Jessica to unravel and the scrolls for Robin. What would either tell them? Amy needed to know? And which cave wall would the writing be on and as to the scrolls, the girls had no idea which one they required. So many unanswered questions, as always in Amy's life.

The girls were soon arriving at the shopping area and looking for the lifts to go down to the caves. Jessica kept stopping to finger through the clothes rails, occasionally picking out a top to coordinate with the jeans she had already picked out.

"Oh, do come on, leave the clothes," Amy said as she pulled Jessica away from the rail.

As much as she wanted to stop and look at clothes herself, Amy needed to get back to find Tom and try to discover more information on her own family history.

Amy had seen the moving, growing family tree in Merlin's big red book, when in Arthur's time and knew there was some mystery about her Great Great Granddad Andrew Duncan.

At the far end, of the second floor of ladies fashions, Amy saw the sign for the lifts, to go down to the caves.

"Come on Jess, over there."

Amy quickly moved towards the lifts in the corner of the shop.

Standing inside the lift, Amy looked at Jessica but no words were spoken between the friends, just a look which said, 'we have to lose these women and children when we get out'. Jessica understood, she knew her friend very well and could guess at what she was thinking.

The lift stopped with a jolt, a computer voice was heard to say "door's opening" the large metal doors opened with a clang, everyone stepped out, the women and children went first as Amy and Jessica held back a little. Once the area was empty the girls made their way towards the other end of the caves, away from the people who had headed in the other direction to the tourist information stand.

Amy and Jessica felt along the sides of the walls; some were rougher than others but all were a golden sandy colour. Where was the darker stone? A few walls had marks scratched into them, as though prisoners had used their nails to leave lines, to count days or months, or maybe even years, Amy thought, as she touched those rough marks made by those ancient   villagers. What were they like, the people Robin had spoken of?

Amy felt a coldness move down her back, she shivered as she saw a black cat run off around the corner and under an arch of stone to disappear; she followed it. Strange, she thought, where did a cat come from? And where did it go?

41

Amy had to crouch to pass under the low arch where the wall became darker and she saw an outline of a man pointing an arrow from his longbow.

"Here Jess, look over here," Amy called to her friend.

Jessica moved closer to Amy to study the carving. Was it of Robin Hood?

Maybe, Amy thought, and used her finger to follow the line of arrows from the one set in the longbow. Where were they pointing? As she touched the wall a line of arrows began to appear, each one following the next around the bend in the wall. That was the very same bend where the cat had run only a few seconds before.

Jessica followed as Amy moved slowly along, touching the wall as she went.

"What have you found?"

"I'm not sure," Amy answered as she looked down to where the arrows had dropped to another carving, this time of a basket holding apples which were all punctured with an arrow.

Amy thought of another old tale she knew, of William Tell and the apple placed on his son's head. The apple which he shot straight through, missing the boy altogether.

Amy's own head was full of tales and mysteries just like that one.

Jessica pushed her toe forward onto a small round stone which protruded out of the lower part of the wall. It looked just like an apple which had fallen from the basket. As she pushed on the stone apple, a grinding sound started to come from the wall. Both girls looked around, afraid other people might hear and would come running to investigate. But there was no one, so Jessica carried on pushing the stone with her toe. She noticed letters forming in the sandstone, only not left to right, not even top to bottom, no, bottom to top, all to spell a word. That stone apple had been a full stop and letters were slowly forming above it. Jessica had to get down on her hands and knees, twist her neck sideways to read the word.

"It's a clue!" Jessica shouted excitedly.

"It's a clue, it's a clue," Amy was excited too. She had loved the clues in her previous adventures.

Jessica was concentrating; what would the words tell her once they had finished forming? Four words were emerging, one above the other, before moving across each other, mixing with each other, why were they doing that? She wondered.

Jessica stood up and watched with Amy; they had to read quickly as the words were fading.

Time.   Line.   Place.   Space.

"Well? What do the words mean?" Amy really needed to know and looked at her friend with a puzzled face.

43

Jessica tried to explain, how some words meant the same and that's why they had mixed with each other. Amy couldn't see how they meant the same. Jessica went on.

"There is a *Timeline*, a *Place* could be a *Space or Time in Space!*"

"And?" Amy asked her next question still with that puzzled look on her face.

"Well, we need to find the *place*, where there is a *space*, and we will need to find a *line*, to move in *time,* to find Tom," Jessica paused then added: 'easy."

"So where's the *place*?" Amy asked.

"Well, I don't know that, yet, we have to find it."

Amy sighed and shook her head.

"This is the *place,* Jess," Amy said standing with her hands resting on her hips and thinking: *I thought you were the person to sort out the puzzles, not me!*

People were coming, the girls could hear children chattering and mums calling after them.

"Quickly Jess, stand with your back to the wall."

The two girls stood to cover the arrows and words as the people passed by, forgetting they were half hidden behind the arch and only their legs could be seen. When the girls turned back to look, the wall was clear of all words and carvings. Now they weren't sure what to do next, they needed to find a *space* because they both felt they were in the right *place*.

A cat screamed, or did it howl? It was definitely not a sweet meow!

That black cat was pushing between the girl's legs and took a nip at Amy's ankle. It had drawn a little spot of blood before it ran off.

"Ouch!" Amy cried out as she bent over to rub her ankle and saw the red blood; she chased the cat away and thought no more of the small pin prick.

"Follow that cat, Jess. I am sure its Cordren's cat."

"Do you think that's a good idea?"

Jessica was rather afraid trouble would be found if they followed that cat! But Amy followed anyway and Jessica thought she had better go too.

"There has to be something else to find."

Amy somehow knew this to be true. She often had a feeling come over her and knew things she could not explain, and she just had to follow her heart.

"Really! Are you sure there is something else?"

Amy told Jessica not to worry. Jessica relaxed and leaned on the cave wall. A crack appeared close by her arm which then slipped and became wedged in the wall, as Jessica tried to move a metal gate banged shut. The girls were trapped down in the caves for the night. Jessica shouted at Amy to help free her arm, but Amy couldn't.

Chapter Six
The other side of the cave's wall

Why had no one checked for the girls when they closed the gates? Because they had sneaked in without a ticket that morning, so no one knew they were down in the caves which had shut early to tourists that day, for what reason Amy didn't know.

"Come here, help me, I'm stuck," Jessica pleaded with Amy and yelled out with pain when Amy pulled at her arm; she was truly stuck in the wall!

"Now what?" Jessica asked, adding, "I can't stop like this all night."

Amy decided she had to somehow make the crack wider, but how? She looked around for anything she could use to smash at the stone wall, but there was nothing!

Just as Amy was beginning to despair she felt something wiggle in her pocket, placing her hand inside she felt the feathers tickle her fingers. Pulling

46

her hand out she found five feathers stuck, one to each finger and one to her thumb. She tossed her hand around, trying to dislodge the feathers and as they slipped off, the feathers flew to settle on the wall of the cave, right next to Jessica's arm. The feathers felt warm to Jessica. The edge of the wall began to turn to dust releasing Jessica's arm which fell like a heavyweight by her side.

The crack was getting wider and wider leaving a hole the girls could look through but it was not quite large enough to walk through.

"We need to go through and see what's hidden there," Amy said excitely.

"How?" Jessica asked looking at her friend's body size and then her own, which was a little larger than Amy's tall thin body. Jessica liked to eat sweets and crisps and it showed. The space in the wall was just too narrow for the girls to enter.

"Watch," Amy said and she took out her new mobile phone which she had been given on her birthday. She touched the screen and pointed it towards the long narrow crack in the wall and took a photo. Then using her thumb and forefinger Amy spread out the picture on the phone's screen and like the picture the cave wall copied and opened up wider.

As Amy had pulled the phone out of her pocket two more golden feathers had fallen out and their warm magic had glowed, just as the bird had glowed on the lawn earlier, glowing from the golden fairy's touch. That was Amy's next thought, the golden fairy had sent the bird.

As those feathers had floated to the sides of Jessica's arm, now another laid itself on the phone to produce more magic, leaving just the one to float around in the air; what was the feather waiting for?

Seven golden feathers were sending out rays of golden light, just like the sun, lighting up a space behind that wall.

"You see, the golden fairy lady sent that bird to help us," Amy was explaining excitedly to Jessica.

"But we don't know if it's safe in that space," Jessica complained some more.

She often did that, complain. Jessica was the worrier while Amy found life exciting, an adventure.

But as Jessica moaned the wall was still opening and Amy smiled, she couldn't wait to see what was on the other side.

"Come on Jess, follow me," Amy said as she dashed through the ever expanding space.

As Amy entered, she saw rows of rolled papers all tied together with red ribbons and piled on a tall rack of shelves.

"Scrolls," Jessica explained as she reached Amy.

"Look at that book!" Amy suddenly shouted out.

There on a middle shelf lay a big red book, just like the ones Amy had seen before. There was one in her father's cellar room, back at her home in Scotland, the book she was never allowed to open and another she had looked in with Merlin in

Arthur's time and the third she had seen in Cordren's den, in the castle of Princess Isabel.

Jessica stood next to Amy looking at the book in amazement for she, too, had seen two books but never knew Amy's father had one. That was a surprise to her and she wondered why her friend had never told her?

There were another twenty shelves, each holding many more scrolls. Very carefully Jessica picked one out, to untie and read while Amy studied the big red book, she had taken from its shelf and was now trying to find out how to open it. She laid the book on the ground while she stopped to rub at her ankle; it was sore from the cat's bite but she didn't notice the red area spreading out around her leg and a green spot building into a blister.

The parchment of the scrolls was so fragile to the touch, Jessica was worried it could fall apart at any moment.

"Which one do we need to take to Robin?" Jessica asked Amy.

"Remember the clues," Amy told her.

"Time.   Line.   Place.   Space."

"Yes?" Jessica was looking at Amy, waiting for her to sort out this puzzle.

"Well, we are in the right *place* and we have found this *space,* behind this wall," Amy reminded her.

"Yes?" Another one-word question came from Jessica who was now staring at Amy with an enquiring face.

Jessica didn't really know what more to say and carried on reading the scroll she held in her hand. Amy then gave in and told her to find the shelf with the scroll from Robin's time.

Amy said no more and read the title of the red book to herself.

'Family,' she read at the top of the book's red cover, the word shining out in silver above a drawing of a silver tree and under this tree, a circle of witches danced. One witch's dress was painted in silver while five more were painted in black.

But what were both these girls looking for?

"Have you not noticed that each shelf covers a time in history?" Amy pointed out to Jessica as she looked from her book.

Amy had seen there were numbers running down the side of the shelves.

Suddenly Amy wanted to read the twenty-first-century scroll and left the red book on the ground to move to the shelf showing the number twenty-one.

"And which shelf did you take that scroll from?" Amy asked Jessica.

"We must not take any after Robin's time," Amy decided and pointed to the shelf of Prince John's time, where just maybe Robin Hood was mentioned.

"Right!" Said Jessica who now understood.

Amy was still tempted to take a scroll from the twenty-first shelf! But no she shouldn't, and she wouldn't, but her future could be in there! She stood and stared at the scrolls on the twenty-first self. She reached out to touch and then pulled back; no she must not go there!. Amy then knew her future may be written but she also knew she had choices in her life to make. Her parents had told her this and those choices could change her life path.

Jessica picked up the partly read scrolls from the ground, replaced them on the shelf and carried on her search. She chose another and laid that one on the ground and called Amy over as she unrolled it to read. Amy noticed the one feather that floated in the air had drifted over above the book, which suddenly flew open. The feather seemed to have a mind of its own and began to move over certain words. It settled on one *line;* Amy read that *line*.

"Jess, look at this," Amy called to her friend.

Taking her school notepad from her pocket Jessica wrote those words down as the feather landed on each one.

The girls gazed down at the words that had been picked out by the fluttering feather. They related to names, Robin, Marion, Cordren, Amy, Katie, Flora, Merlin and Arthur and many others, all going back to Amy's great, great grandparents and beyond. Some names meant nothing to Amy and then there was the Golden Lady and Merlin's name too. The book's cover had read 'Family'. Was it a mix of people's family history inside, or was it all Amy's family?

"And? What did these names tell the girls?" Amy asked her friend who normally worked out puzzles so easily, only today she seemed confused. Why was that? Amy looked disappointed and could not see how these people could all be from one family.

"There has to be a connection," Jessica eventually said and the two girls looked at each other before deciding they had to find a way out of the caves and go back to Robin, taking this one scroll and the book with them. But as Jessica rolled and tied the red ribbon back around the scroll's centre it jumped from her hands and flew back to the shelf where it had sat for so many hundreds of years.

"No, we can't remove anything from here," Amy said at that moment. "We need a copy; I will use my phone again."

Amy pulled her phone from her pocket once more as Jessica fought with the scroll she was pulling hard to get off the shelf and when she had managed that it kept wiggling in her hands until she told the scroll, she only wanted to read it. The scroll seemed to understand and relaxed. Hanging in mid-air the scroll let Jessica pull at the red ribbon which untied itself and gently floated to the ground. Amy took a photo of all the fancy writing on the scroll before it rolled itself up once more, waited for the ribbon to leap from the ground and re-tie itself around its middle. Slowly the scroll drifted through the air and over to the shelf, found a space, gave a little wiggle and settled itself between the rest of the scrolls, where it might lay for hundreds of years to come.

The girls had been so engrossed in their finding they hadn't noticed the wall had closed behind them, to keep those scrolls secret.

Jessica had had another great idea.

"Use both your time and light on your phone."

Amy set her phone on the date when Robin Hood was supposed to have lived and pointed the line of light which she had also turned on to point around this *space* they were in.

Was anything changing? Yes, there in the corner, the wall was much darker and breaking down, crumbling away as though time was moving it back, to when the caves were a different shape.

A dim light poured through where the sandstone rock had disintegrated into a pile of dust. The girls edged their way forward. It was dusk outside and the shops had disappeared. They gingerly stepped forward, to the edge of a river where mist floated and curled over its surface.

"It's the River Trent," Jessica stated as if she really knew where they were, "and look there's a row boat hiding in the reeds."

There was also a castle standing in the moonlight behind them on top of those caves, the castle that kept disappearing, Nottingham castle. Why does that stone castle keep doing that? Coming and going! Amy thought. Was it something to do with the passage of time which she and Jessica had moved through? Then her phone went dead, well, of course, it would, her phone never works in her adventures, her fantasy world, a different time.

They were back in time!

Chapter Seven
Back to Robin

"Let's go to the forest," Jessica suggested and ran off, not noticing Amy was limping now from the pain in her ankle. Amy called her back and pointed to the boat.

"Let's use that boat."

Amy needed to sit down and rest her ankle.

"Good idea," Jessica said and stopped to pull it clear of the reeds for Amy to step in.

The river ran slowly along with the boat and its oars used by Jessica, they were going nowhere fast. The full moon gave an eerie feel to the night as it moved behind drifting clouds which made creepy shapes through the gaps of trees where owls sat to hoot.

Suddenly the little boat rocked from side to side. A dripping hand shot up from the water, Jessica screamed so loud, Amy scolded her. The wet hand grabbed hold of the side of the boat which tipped slightly sideways. Jessica screamed again but covered her mouth this time, her eyes staring wide open with fear. She was sure the boat was going to topple over and they would land up in the murky water, to be eaten by a monster.

"Oh be quiet," a voice was heard to say. "It's only me," and Katie's head popped up from the river.

"What are you doing in there?" Amy asked with a sigh of relief.

"I have been looking for Thomas and a way into that oak tree. I thought perhaps through its roots."

"Why? Is Tom in a tree?" Amy asked another one of her questions.

"Maybe, I don't really know where Thomas is but Cordren is in there; she may have him."

Amy told Katie she needed to get back to Robin, to find the field where they had been with Mr Woodstock and on to the forest but it was taking them so long as the river flowed so slowly.

Katie held her magic camera up from the water and pointed it at the little boat, she clicked on a button from down the camera's side and in a flash the little row boat's front end tipped up, throwing the two girls backward. The backend of the boat now sat low in the water just as a speed boat would and with the front pointing up towards the night sky it took off at such a speed, just like a speedboat would splashing through a river or on the sea.

"Hang on," Katie shouted after the two girls and within seconds the girls were at the field.

Katie in the meantime swam deep into that murky river, into the darkness after waving her tail at the girls. She followed the river to where tree roots reached out for a drink. She wanted to get inside that oak tree and she thought the roots would be the best way to go.

Amy and Jessica clambered from the boat and climbed the wet muddy, slippery river bank into the field, where the archery had taken place only hours before and there they found two arrows sticking in the ground. Both were left from the class practice time, only there were no bows to shoot the arrows from. Mr Woodstock must have taken them back to the building they were staying in, Amy thought.

"Let's just throw the arrows together," was Jessica's next suggestion before Amy asked one of her many questions.

"How is that going to work?" Amy still managed to ask!

Amy stopped to think; she still had a few golden feathers left in her pocket.

"Here take these golden feathers, Jess and lay them over the arrows."

Jessica didn't ask why, she knew Amy would have a good reason to do this.

A thick misty fog started to roll over the grassy field. Neither girl could see clearly their arrows travelling into the fog. But as the fog swirled and cleared the golden fairy lady came into view from around the back of a tree.

"Oh good, you have returned," she said as she noticed the two arrows covered in golden feathers sticking in the bark of the tree.

"Yes!" Amy and Jessica said together, so happy to be in the right *place* and *time* with the golden fairy before them and ready to help. Amy went on to ask after Tom.

"He's fine," she said and led the girls into the forest to stand under that huge, old English Oak tree with the hollow in its trunk. But wasn't this the tree Amy had seen on the front of that big red book, the one she had left behind? She wondered if some of her family were over eight hundred years old like this tree? Surely not! She must get home and look in her father's book.

"Have you any of the golden feathers left with you?" The golden fairy asked.

The two girls looked at each other, had they any left? Yes, Amy had a few and Jessica too.

"What about the lace and the scroll?" Katie asked as she popped her head out from inside the tree.

"Well no, not quite," Amy said in a rather sheepish voice, "but we do have a photo of the lace and of a scroll, on my phone. Did you find Tom in the tree?"

"Show me," Katie asked, "and no I didn't find Tom."

Amy moved closer to the tree and handed over her phone with the photos stored in its memory, but would the phone work? Would it show the two photos here in this time?

Katie quickly attached the phone into a slot in the top of her magic camera, clicked two different buttons from down its side and immediately a piece of lace began to appear from a lace hook which hung from the camera. The hook dashed about weaving a cream patterned piece of lace. When it was finished the lace fell to the ground as a small roll of paper now started to be ejected from the top of the camera; it was a copy of the information from the scroll.

"Wow!" Jessica said as she bent down to pick up the lace. Amy held the paper curling out from this magical camera.

"How did you do that?" And just as Jessica finished her words the phone went dead again. Well, of course, it would, Amy was in one of her adventures, where mobiles don't work.

"We need to get these to Robin," Katie said as the ground began to move.

A huge tree root wiggled its way slowly from behind Katie and towards her feet, it grabbed out, it pulled and twisted around her ankles. Katie fell with a thud to the ground. She yelled she was being dragged along towards the hollow in the trunk of the tree; she clung to the ground, her fingers grasping at the earth but it made no difference, she disappeared inside the tree. The girls could do nothing but watch, it all happened so quickly.

"Help," Katie still screamed out and then she was gone and all was quiet.

"I have to get inside that tree," Amy called out in despair and the fairy placed her wings around her to comfort Amy.

Chapter Eight
Thomas

All this time Thomas had been riding with Robin who had gone back to the lake to find him.

Robin wanted to find Marion now he had Thomas by his side and help her become a real person again. That would be difficult as a spell by Cordren's mother had been placed over her after Marion's parents had burnt down Cordren's family den. That was after an old uncle of Cordren had taken Marion's family lands. It was two families being very silly over a disagreement that had dragged on and on. If only both families had sat down and talked with each other an arrangement could have been drawn up and there would have been no need for all the troubles. But people can be awkward sometimes, Robin had heard his father say and no one wins in the end!

As the years had passed by Marion's parents had died as Robin's had too and both were alone, but Robin was strong. Sadly Marion was not and was left to fade away after that spell was placed over her which had taken her warmer inner self, the unseen power of life.

And so Robin with the help of the fairy lady and now Katie with the magic camera would both try to sort the Marion problem out. But first they had to find Cordren's family and that was where Amy could help. Because if Cordren knew Amy was here, she would show herself and Robin could find the red book of spells she always carried with her and save Marion.

As Robin had searched he had found the old oak tree with a hollow centre because Amy had sent the arrow into it and that had been the sign, the tale Robin had been told to watch for all his life.

Now he had found Cordren and her family in their den, well for now anyway, because they were always on the move. Cordren's family didn't want to be caught and burnt at the stake before the King, as witches were then and so they kept moving.

So Robin had befriended Thomas, after finding him, he could tell Amy's friend was completely at a loss as to what was happening to him.

Now he wanted to save Marion.

*

Thomas had enjoyed his short time with Robin, riding the Nottinghamshire lands on a fine horse, Katie's black stallion, named Cole, as he had enjoyed riding with his grandfather. He had spent time asking Robin questions about who he was and where he was and what he had learned from Robin meant Thomas had many, many more questions for Amy when he saw her, that was for sure

.

Chapter Nine
All back together in Sherwood Forest

The girls gathered close to Robin as he rode up with Thomas. They were in shock at what had happened to Katie. Robin asked where she was and was also surprised but reassured the girls they would get inside that tree and rescue her.

Picking up the copy of the scroll and the lace which Katie had left behind, they read together. It ended at the year they were in. It told of the strength and goodness of a boy named Robin who would become a leader of men one day.

Amy smiled at Jessica, they both knew the future. Robin looked puzzled.

Amy pointed to the names sewn into the lace picture around the castle and asked for the copy of the scroll to be laid close to the lace on the grass. The information matched perfectly with all the names and the castle.

"What can you tell from these?" Amy asked Robin just as that black cat scampered over the paper, tearing it with its pointed razor sharp claws as it ran.

"Darkness come here," a cackling voice was heard calling after that cat, a voice from within the oak tree's hollow, where Katie had been dragged only moments before.

The cat had dashed passed the group of youngsters and was now inside the tree with part of the scroll still caught between his sharp claws. That crackling voice was heard again, it was Cordren's voice thanking her cat, Darkness.

"Well done, my beauty."

Unseen by everyone outside of the tree, Cordren was stroking her cat which purred in a strange sort of way inside the hollow.

"No," Amy screamed and ran after the cat, only to fall down a massive hole left by the tree root.

Jessica dashed after Amy, but the hole had been sealed by Cordren moving a massive acorn seed with one of her spells, an acorn big enough to sit on and now no one was going to enter that tree, well not through that way!

Jessica slumped to the ground, looking at that acorn. She was so frightened for her friend and Katie too.

"We will find the girls," Thomas said.

He had been at the lakeside after the girls had left him there when they had returned to their own *time* but Robin had gone back for him and now Thomas wanted to help Robin and the other boys he had been riding with.

The words,

Time,   Line,   Place,   Space,

kept churning over in Jessica's mind and now Amy was missing, in a *space* (the hollow of a tree) in (Robin's) *time* of which Jessica knew little. There was a *line* left on the ground where the tree root had dragged Katie. But what was this *place*? Oh, Jessica was having real trouble with this puzzle. Then she noticed the big red book had been dropped close by the tree, but by whom? She hadn't brought it with her and she hadn't seen Amy with it.

"Look what's come from the cave," she called over to the golden fairy.

Cordren had dropped the book when she dropped her cat to rip the scroll laying on the ground, as she had flown overhead to the tree. She didn't want anyone reading that scroll! But as Jessica walked over to pick the book up it jumped into the air, flapped its outer covers and flew into the branches of the tree where Cordren sat before disappearing into the tree with the book under her cloak.

"Now we have lost the book too, as well as Katie and Amy, we are not doing very well, are we?" Jessica said and the fairy seemed to be doing nothing to help.

The connection between Amy, Cordren, Katie, and the golden fairy lady were all in that book, just as their names were all together on a piece of lace and written on a scroll. There had to be a reason for that and then there was the name Merlin; why would he be mentioned when like King Arthur and

64

Robin Hood they were only legends? How did he fit into Amy's family? It just got weirder all the time and now Jessica asked as many questions and wanted as many answers as Amy wanted.

Jessica must save Amy from the tree and Cordren.

Robin must find Marion and break the spell.

There was a lot to do!

Chapter Ten
Inside the hollow tree

Amy found herself sitting in the basement of a tree house, only this tree house was underground not in a tree top.

Amy had been feeling sleepy, her ankle and now part of her leg hurt. She pulled her jeans up to rub at her lower leg and could see why it hurt so much. The skin was red and green blisters had formed, one was weeping green and purple gunge from a small pin size hole; it was this poison that made Amy feel so sleepy.

As Amy sat there the tree shook from side to side, as though it was unhappy.

She pulled herself up, to stand and look for a way up to that second floor where she could now see the red book waited, she so wanted to read it.

There were no stairs but there was a thick purple rope dangling from floor to floor. Was that her way up? Maybe, and Amy soon found herself tugging at the end of the rope and thinking she could try and climb as she had done on a rope in school, in her gymnastics lesson.

As she looked up she could see other floors lying at different angles and levels while in the centre of this wide gap the rope dangled. It went from the dirt covered ground where Amy stood to a ceiling made of clear glass, where she could see the sky.

Amy stood close by a pit of flames licking round a black pot containing a bubbling green mixture. Smoke curled from the fire and drifted up towards that glass dome to leave the room by a narrow hole in the glass roof.

Amy thought she must leave this tree, find her way out, only she didn't feel too well. Her ankle was so very sore now and rubbing the area she noticed green and purple pus squirted out over her hand.

"Ouch," she said quietly to herself as she pulled a tissue from her pocket and dabbed at the mess trickling from the spot.

A golden feather flew from her pocket with the tissue. Amy quickly grabbed the feather back, but it tickled the inside of her hand and wiggled its way out, to float down to her weeping ankle, where it settled on her sore place. As Amy looked down at her leg she noticed the redness retreating back towards her ankle as her leg slowly returned to a normally pale skin colour.

The feather was wiggling like a worm over the green and purple mess, it seemed to be sucking it up before spitting it out as golden bubbles which soon burst and disappeared into the air. Amy was beginning to feel better and knew the golden fairy had touched that feather with her kindness, a feather that had come from her golden bird who had settled on the lawn.

Amy shivered as she stood and limped on her poorly leg which still felt a little weak. She held the rope, she pulled on it, it held tight to whatever it was knotted to above. Amy felt it was safe to climb. With a struggle, she made her climb to the second floor.

This floor held a table and a stool where a huge grey rat with long, twitching whiskers sat to eat at stale bread. Amy shivered some more at the sight of it nibbling mouldy food. Close by, a wooden podium stood holding that big red book. A black Crow was perched menacingly by the side of this book. This Crow kept bobbing its grey head up and down and with a sinister squawk, words came from its long grey, pointed beak.

"We have you now, Amy," it said, and it spread out its wings and flapped them which scared the rat which jumped down from its eating and scurried off across the wooden floor into a corner to sit and watch.

Amy didn't like the look of this bird or the disappearing rat, either.

There was a third floor above. It was hard for Amy to see from where she stood but she could just manage to see a black cat, its front paws, and head hanging over the side, where the edge of covers were falling from what she thought must be a bed, He moved slightly to glare down at Amy with his evil eyes while a hissing sound came from between his pointed teeth, but the cat could not reach her. Amy shivered again, yet she was sweating as well. Some of that poison was still making Amy feel unwell. She wished someone would come and find her.

Amy recovered her thoughts and looked around to see pictures of Cordren's family hanging on the wall, the witches she, Arthur and Merlin had once battled, on her school trip to a magical land last autumn.

The eyes from these pictures seemed to move and follow Amy as she moved from one picture to another. Cordren's father, Thunderbolt sent out an evil look from his black eyes. Reganner, his wife looked over at him with her deep midnight blue eyes and a grey twisted smile came from her mouth. Their three children sat together all in one picture which hung beneath their parents, their eyes all sparkled green as though they were not so evil witches. Cordren sat in the middle, almost smiling, with her sister, Morgana to the right and her brother, Mordred to her left. He looked more serious than his two sisters and all three wore black witch's hats, the brims green as were the inside of their black cloaks, all matching their eyes.

Amy moved over to the podium now the Crow had flown off to the floor above. She opened the big red book and it let out a squeal, as though in pain. Amy flipped over the pages which sent out a sudden alarm signal, with each turn the alarm got higher, hurting Amy's ears.

Amy covered her ears with her hands as the bird flew back down to frighten her, making her duck down as it flew low over her head. The cat watched from above and still hissed as the bird flew off again; was it going to find a witch and bring one back, which one would it be?

Amy was flicking through the pages quickly now when a sudden scream was heard and the tree shook once more. Amy toppled over on her bad leg as the tree wobbled from side to side and the book shut its self with a thud!

Suddenly Cordren was standing over Amy; what was she going to do with her? For so long she had tried to trap Amy and Katie and now she had Amy in her power and she was unsure about what to do, now she had her. A feeling Cordren hadn't expected, why was that? Was it her parents that had filled her head with vengeance? Maybe it was, something from their family history, only she didn't know what that could possibly be. Every time she went to read a page from that big red book to try and find out, it had shut itself tight, almost cutting off Cordren's fingers on one occasion and now Amy's too.

The book seemed to have a mind of its own unless Cordren was using the pages for cooking spells, then it stayed open.

Cordren suddenly didn't want to hurt Amy anymore. But why was that? She frowned, making wrinkles show up on her forehead as she stared at Amy.

A green flash lit up the inside of the tree; Thunderbolt had arrived in a whirl of lime green mist.

"What are you doing girl," he screamed at Cordren, his daughter.

"Nothing, father."

Reganner entered the tree now to stand tall against her husband.

"Leave the girl alone, she doesn't understand."

"Understand what?" Cordren asked her parents as she moved away from Amy now, to stare at her mother.

No more was said before the tree began to speak.

"She is coming," the tree whispered in a rustling sound, as though afraid to mention a name.

The three witches spun around. They, too knew a dreaded force was coming, but who was coming? Cordren didn't know nor did Amy, who stood very still, as the cat watched and waited too, But where had that bird and rat gone to?

Chapter Eleven
Outside the tree

Daylight had arrived and Amy's friends had gathered by the oak tree, still wondering how they were going to find their friend and Katie.

Suddenly horses' hooves were heard thundering through the forest.

"Quick! To the trees," Robin commanded his friends.

The golden fairy fluttered her wings and rose above the tree tops to hide in the sun's golden rays which were streaming down to earth. No one would see her there.

Now Jessica was left with Robin and both were unsure as to what they should do next.

Suddenly those thundering hooves had arrived, bringing horses with soldiers on their backs. The commander shouted orders to his men, to walk Robin and Jessica to the castle.

Both were pulled and pushed roughly forward, both boy and girl stumbled as they walked. The pair fell many times on the uneven ground, only to be pulled up by a horseman wearing the uniform of Prince John's guard. Thankfully it wasn't too long before the castle came into view. Jessica recognised the sandstone caves supporting the castle, the place she and Amy had been in only hours before, although it had actually been hundred of years into the future! Robin knew they were heading for the prison, where many of the older people from his village had been taken. Jessica remembered the scratches on the cave's walls, where prisoners had left their marks, to count the time they had spent there. How long would she be there?

Robin was placed in a cell with other boys of his own age and a few old men who did not stir from their sleep. The younger men had been put to work outside, digging a moat around the castle. In the next cell was Jessica and she had thought it was empty, but there was one tiny girl hunched up in the far corner. She looked very pale with black curly hair in a tangled mess, almost like her own. She wore a dirty white blouse and a ragged brown skirt.

"What's your name?" Jessica asked her.

"Marion," she replied in a very low and shy voice.

"Wow, really, do you know Robin Hood?" Jessica's next question came for this girl. Jessica was getting like her friend Amy, always asking questions!

"No, I have heard of the boy. He is supposed to be a good person, but I have not met him."

"Yes, he is good and will be a great man one day." Jessica thought she had said too much. Marion was supposed to become his love when she was older if any of the legends was true. This girl was very odd, though. Jessica now realised as Marion came closer she could see right through her.

Jessica jumped back in fright, her eyes open wide; she was a ghost after all! Was she the ghost she had seen on her first day in Nottingham?

The next thing Jessica heard was the banging of cell gates and a man's deep voice ordering Robin to move out. Jessica ran to watch as Robin was pushed along the small space between the cave wall and her cell, towards steps, where earlier she had come down in a lift with Amy from the shops above.

"Where are you taking me?" Robin said very loudly. He wanted Jessica to hear, so she would know where to find him, as he was sure the golden fairy would come to rescue them both very soon.

"Shut up and move along. Prince John wants to question you," the soldier yelled back at Robin.

Jessica sat down, hoping Robin would return, but he took so long that she fell asleep with the boredom, sitting with her back to the wall away from that ghostly looking girl and when she woke again she wondered where she was for just a moment and when she remembered, that girl named Marion had vanished from the cell. Jessica looked around, where was that ghostly figure?

Jessica heard a voice, it was a girl's shy voice, quietly calling her, telling her to come closer to the bars of her cell.

Jessica jumped up and was startled to see the ghostly figure of Marion standing on the other side of the bars of her cell.

"How did you get out there?" Jessica asked.

Marion never gave an explanation but did tell her to take a feather from her pocket and to hold it under a soldier's nose.

"When he comes back," she said.

Jessica looked puzzled, why should she do that?

And like a ghost, Marion disappeared. How odd, Jessica thought; what could a single golden feather do? And how did she know about the feathers anyway? But Jessica took one from her pocket. She was ready and waiting.

It wasn't long before footsteps were heard returning. Who would it be coming around the corner? Hopefully, Robin, Jessica thought.

But it was not a soldier but a hunched back person wearing a black hooded cloak from where grey hair poked out around a grey wrinkled face with a pointed nose. An old woman with a walking stick threw back her cloak to show its grey lining draped over a long black ragged dress and black short boots. Jessica had no idea who she was but she should have been scared, for the old woman knew Cordren. Jessica would soon find out this person was Cordren's grandmother. Marion followed the old woman who had hold of her wrist, which was fading.

Jessica had never seen Marion looking so transparent.

"Help me," Marion cried weakly.

"What can I do?" Jessica asked.

"Cordren's Grandmother has my inner self, she took my warm feeling from my chest with a wicked spell and unless I can receive it back into my body, I will be left to walk that lawn forever as a ghost."

Marion said no more, she could only follow the old woman. Marion was fading more and more as she walked on, soon she would die. She had used all her strength to get a message to the golden fairy before this witch recaptured her. It had been many months since Marion was taken away from the castle where she had lived as an orphan and now it appeared she would need the help of Jessica and her friends to save her and get her noticed by Robin as a pretty young girl who one day he might fall in love with. Marion did not want to be some grey ugly old ghost.

Robin returned with his soldier guarding him as Marion and her captor vanished from the cave. Jessica had to be quick. She took the feather and rushed to the bars of her cell, called out to the soldier to come over.

"What girl, what do you want?" the soldier yelled at her as he gripped hold of a bar.

Jessica pushed her hand through the bars and waved the golden feather under his nose. He sneezed and staggered forward hitting his head on the metal bars of the cell. Robin pushed him over, he fell to the ground, knocked out. Robin grabbed the huge ring of keys from his belt. He fumbled to find the right key for Jessicas's cell before unlocking it. She ran out and both looked for a way out of the caves.

Robin stopped to free the old men from their cells. Jessica must wait for him and as she did she threw another golden feather into the air and wished for the golden fairy lady to appear.

It was not long before a draft was felt, dust flew up into the air, a golden body was forming and very soon a spinning fairy was hovering just above the ground before them.

"Yes, can I help you?" she said in her kind voice.

The golden fairy lady always helped good people.

The soldier stirred but did not wake.

"Come on with me, Jess, hold my hands, shut your eyes, you too Robin," the golden fairy instructed the pair just before she began to spin again.

The group of three were spinning inside the caves at one moment and the next they found themselves outside in the forest close to the oak tree.

Chapter Twelve
The Oak Tree

A whirl of golden dust came to settle just before the oak tree. Jessica and Robin were becoming whole again and feeling very dizzy.

Jessica let go of the fairy's hand and stumbled closer to the tree trunk to look inside but the hole was still sealed by that huge acorn.

Now they must find some other way into that tree to find their friends.

There was a rustling in the branches above and out popped small smiling faces, Robin's friends, and Thomas. Once they were sure there was no one else around they all jumped down and greeted Robin, Jessica, and the fairy.

"We have to get inside that tree," Robin told his friends who were happy to see him and know that he had escaped the prison.

"Up there, I saw a hole, in the thickest branch, that leads inside the top part of the tree, but it's very small, we will never get through," Thomas told everyone.

"We could try," Robin replied.

"Yes let's try," the shout went up from all the boys.

The boys climbed back up the big old tree as the golden fairy floated up to the top, holding Jessica by her arm.

Jessica became very excited because she remembered how she had so wanted to fly with this fairy when Amy flew over a rainbow. That was when all three girls had saved Princess Isabel in a previous adventure and now she was flying too!

"Yaaaaaaaaa," Jessica sang out happily as her feet left the ground.

There were many branches growing from the top of this old tree and now each boy sat on one to look at each other, all wondering if they could really get inside and if so what would they find? Who would they find?

Although the golden fairy lady could have made it easy for all the youngsters, by telling them what to do, or use her fairy magic as Katie did with her camera, she knew they had to learn to think for themselves, just as all parents tell their children and if they needed help they must not be too shy to ask for help. Use your brain, think the problem through, Jessica remembered her parents telling her and she often did so when working out her own puzzles and those in Amy's adventures. People are here to help, her mother had said but also you must make your own decisions and learn from them.

Jessica wanted to know if anyone had seen Amy and was about to ask for help in finding her when the tree swung its branches wildly about, trying to dislodge its visitors; the boys hung on tightly. But it wasn't Jessica and her friends the tree wanted to remove, it was Cordren and all her family because the tree knew the old wicked grandmother was coming.

On the very top branch sat the Crow from Cordren's hideout. It was making a dreadful sound from its open beak which pointed skywards, calling other Crows to flock together and help chase off these boys. The huge black mass of menacing crows flew down, all pointing their sharp beaks at the boys sitting in the tree and, leading this dark mass, was a figure cloaked in black and wearing a witch's hat. It was Cordren's grandmother, in fact, that grey-headed crow was no bird but the grandmother witch of all witches. She was able to change her body into a bird's body as her husband could change his into animals.

As the tree lashed about the birds circled around and the youngsters hung on.

The golden fairy came to the rescue, flapping her transparent wings into a frenzy, sending out clouds of golden fairy dust which would destroy any witch it touched. The birds took off before the golden dust landed. Had a spot of dust fell on them they would have disintegrated too because they were very young witches, brought here from afar.

The old witch waved her magic fingernail and sparks flew out across a branch, she muttered a few magic words at that hole in the branch and then began to dive down to enter. Once she was inside the boys followed before the hole could close again.

The golden dust settled on the leaves of the tree turning them into sparkling golden colours as though autumn had arrived early. The tree gave out a gentle moan of warmth, a happy sound and on its trunk, the bark showed a twisted smile below two small holes where an owl's eyes shone out. The tree looked like it had a wide open mouth, with eyes above, the tree had made a smiley face from the holes in its bark. Yes, the tree was happy and was inviting the boys in to save Amy. The old grandmother witch, without thinking, had made the hole large enough for all to get through.

*

Robin was the first to enter and shouted to his friends to follow him in. But Robin should never have shouted so loud.

Prince John and his soldiers were close by and rode up to stop beneath the tree. Jessica had been the last to enter and had slipped, leaving one of her legs dangling out of the hole which was shrinking all the time and would soon squeeze her leg, but she could not move and give the hiding place away. She gasped and covered her mouth with her hand, scared she had been seen or heard by a soldier or that her leg would become trapped as her arm had in the wall.

The rear soldier did turn to look but dismissed his thinking that he had seen or heard anything.

Everyone sat very still not daring to move as the Prince searched the area below, but he and his men could see no one and soon galloped off.

The fairy had flown down and around the soldier's heads to distract them from their search before flying off towards the castle.

"Follow that witch, we will burn her at the stake," Prince John commanded his soldiers. No man believed in fairies, so this lady could only be a witch.

"Help!" A tiny voice was heard and it wasn't Jessica because she had now pulled her leg up. So where did the little voice come from?

Everyone looked around. The words came from a fading Marion who had been dropped by the old witch as she flew over the tree and now Marion hung dangerously from the branch the boys had entered. There was only her head and that one clinging hand showing, other than a blouse and skirt which seemed to hang over nothing, as her body and legs had faded away.

"Don't disappear!" Robin said as he popped his head back out of the hole, but Marion couldn't help herself.

"Save me, Robin," she cried out, but now only in a whimper. She could not shout; she was fading fast as her other hand reached out to Robin, to pull her into the tree.

"What can we do?" Robin asked in a distressed voice.

The fairy lady had flown off and still, there was no sign of Katie and her magic camera to help her.

Robin took command, telling all who looked at him for an answer.

"We must go right inside and find Amy and Katie."

Of course, Robin and his friends knew nothing of Cordren's family. Only Jessica knew her family meant trouble.

Robin led the way, he took a few steps into a tunnel leading to a slide to slip down to other areas of the tree trunk. Robin went tumbling down first followed by the rest of the boys who all landed in a heap on top of Robin.

There they all sat, rubbing heads, arms, and legs but no one was badly hurt and they could all stand, but where were they? None of the boys had ever been inside a tree before. And Marion was still slowly fading away outside. Robin would go back for her later, as soon as he found his way out of the tree with Amy and his task complete.

Chapter Thirteen
Inside a Tree with a Family of Witches

The youngsters had landed in a heap right behind Cordron and her family. Only the sister, Morgana, was missing.

"What do you want with me?" Amy asked Cordren who stood back, saying nothing as her father, Thunderbolt, moved across to the big red book and slammed it shut. He was letting no one look inside.

Thunderbolt grabbed roughly at Amy's arm and pulled her up; she wobbled on her legs.

"You have been nothing but trouble ever since the day you were born," he said.

What did he mean? Amy wondered. She hadn't known him.

Thunderbolt had hardly finished talking when he was rushed upon from behind by Robin, his friends pounced on the other witches who had stood with their backs to the boys. Jessica ran straight over to Amy and threw her arms around her shoulders.

"Oh, Amy are you all right?" Jessica was smiling so much it almost hurt her face.

Amy felt dazed as she looked at Jessica. Robin took command of the situation and removed the witches broomsticks from their hands. He was making sure they could not fly off. His friends were running around the group of witches with the purple rope Amy had managed to climb up earlier. They had pulled it down and had soon tied the witches together.

The rat, the cat, and the Crow were nowhere to be seen, where had all these creatures vanished to?

Amy asked Jessica where Katie was and had she seen Thomas, who she hadn't noticed was helping the boys capture the witches?

No one seemed to know where Katie was, not even the boys, who had joined in the conversation but Thomas came up to Amy and hugged her.

"Oh, Tom are you alright?"

"Yes I am fine, are you?"

"Yes."

Suddenly the red book flew open of its own accord, it took flight from the podium, flapping its heavy red covers as though it had turned into an aeroplane.The white inner pages kept flipping over, back and forth they moved throwing out words to float in the air.

"No!" Thunderbolt screamed out at the book. "Lie down, lie still, shut your covers," the witch shouted his commands, but the book took no notice and carried on flying around the room sending out its letters, that now rained down to form words. Thunderbolt no longer had his broomstick to fly on and catch the book or to cast a spell or to control the book that held the spells and secrets.

Amy so wanted the information hiding from her in that book, how could she catch it?

Everyone was watching this book fly around in circles as they covered their heads with their arms while ducking down out of its way. Only Amy reached up to try and grab it, but she was never going to succeed.

No one took the time to see the rat or cat reappear at their feet or the Crow fly in, to sit on a rafter high up in the tree house or the golden bird from the lawn which was chasing the black curly letters left floating in the air, because everything was happing at once and all so very fast, it was just too much for the tree. It shuddered to make everyone topple over, even the cat, whose four legs gave way while its tail bushed out to twice its size, as it always did when it was cross and the rat's beady eyes now glowed red with anger instead of the deep black of terror.

The tree house began to rattle, its wooden beams creaked, pots fell off shelves and the witch's paintings on the walls swung from side to side. The three floors began to fall and crashed down upon each other, dust clouds rolled in the air, boys were coughing, two birds chirped and a cat hissed. Robin and his friends fell as did the witches, still tied together, in a bundle. They rolled around and screamed out worthless spells.

The pressure of the tree house falling sent dust rolling towards that huge acorn, causing it to shoot out like a rocket from its resting place. That left the hollow clear at the base of the tree for Robin to race out of, as did his friends who were followed by Jessica and Amy. The witches were left lying in a bundle, to roll out along the ground, but still there was no sign of Katie.

It took only a few seconds for everyone to come to their senses before Jessica asked:

"what was that all about?"

"I can tell you." It was the golden fairy talking. She had returned and as she floated down she explained that the bird had the words in his beak to tell the story from the book and it was the book that had wrecked the inner tree.

"It does? It did?" Asks Amy.

The golden bird had collected the letters from the air.

The bird flew overhead in circles, but oh no! The crow was chasing after the golden bird, swooping up and diving down through the air and now both birds were heading towards the castle. Flying as fast as their wings could carry them, while still diving and soaring back up into the clouds they chased each other, like two old Spitfire fighter war planes which the girls had seen in films. Just as the two birds reached the huge turret in the center of the castle, close to the grass area which in Amy's time would be known as a lawn, the two birds changed into two different beings. The crow had flapped its wings which now turned into a black cloak with a grey lining, the grandmother witch, and the golden bird became another golden fairy, but she had silver wings not transparent like the golden fairy Amy knew.

"No," Amy sighed as she sat down feeling deflated at losing the words which may tell her story from her past.

"Now what?" Jessica said standing over Amy while looking in disbelief in the direction of the castle which neither girls could see.

"Come on we have to get back to the castle," Robin said as though he and his friends were the only ones who could still see it. The group of boys without Thomas dashed off, running as fast as they could as their horses had been rounded up by Prince John's soldiers and taken away.

"Why didn't Robin wait for us?" Amy asked another question.

"Because it was the ghostly body of Marion the crow was carrying in his claws," The fairy lady said. "Robin couldn't wait."

"And how are we going to find the castle when we cannot even see it? And why can't we see it?" Amy asked two question now.

She was suffering from strange pictures floating past her eyes.

"Amy, are you all right?" Jessica asked her.

"I will be," she said. "Only I wish Katie was here."

Suddenly Katie was standing in front of Amy. She had been down in the roots of the tree when the tree house came crashing down. She had decided to take a picture of herself and snap, she had transported herself outside.

"Oh, Katie you're here," Jessica screamed with joy and Amy smiled.

Thomas sat head in hands looking so cross with himself for not going with Robin. He wanted to be in control of his life. After all, he was a boy and one day would be a man. He wanted to know what to do in any given situation, be strong and so far that was the last thing he had been.

Katie could read his mind and sat down along side him. Touching Thomas's arm she softly started to talk with him.

"Now, Tom, there is much you have to learn and you are still young. Some things you have already learned with Amy, but cannot remember or understand but you will in time and you will be Amy's partner in her future adventures as you have before and you will be a great asset to Amy and the world one day."

Thomas looked hard at Katie. Who was this girl and what was she talking about and how come she had a tail when her legs became wet?

"What are you talking about?" Thomas had found his voice.

"When it is the new year and Amy becomes a teenager you must be with her."

"Why?" He frowned.

"She will need you, it's very important. That's all I can tell you for now."

As Katie finished talking the golden fairy lady flew down and Thomas looked up in surprise. He was thinking about all these people around him; they acted out some very strange things and he had thought Amy was strange, sometimes, but he had kept quiet about that, not like that boy named Sam from school.

"You go on, we will meet you at the castle," Katie told the fairy. "Find your golden mother."

That golden bird was, in fact, the golden fairy lady's mother who had silver wings unlike her with her transparent wings. As the fairies aged, which took a lot, lot longer than Amy or Jessica to age, their wings would turn from transparent to silver to gold, like a grandmother fairy.

"The castle will show itself when it's ready for us to see it," Amy told her friends.

"We can use the magic of the camera, now Robin and those boys have left us," Katie told the two girls.

The fewer people who knew of the camera's magic the better.

Everyone had forgotten about the bundle of witches tied up with the purple rope and when Jessica did remember, she quickly twisted her head to see the cat and the rat struggling to free Cordren and her family.

The cat had clawed its way through the rope as the rat had chewed and left ragged ends.

"They're getting away," Amy shouted.

The broomsticks which Robin had left on the ground had been picked up by Cordren's missing sister, Morgana, who had returned to help with her family's escape.

"We will return," Thunderbolt screamed back, as he and his family flew off towards the castle.

Just one witch hesitated, Cordren. Something was troubling her and she hovered above Amy, not wanting to leave her. Why was that? Normally Cordren would worry only about herself and the fairy dust which might settle on her, for she knew that dust could kill her and her family.

"Are you all right?" Cordren asked when looking down at Amy through different eyes, now, eyes which showed concern.

"Yes, I am fine, it's just I keep getting flashing images in my head. I have so many questions, are you really related to me?" Amy asked Cordren in a very calm voice.

"I have actually been protecting you from my family," Cordren quietly replied. "Read the book. The names from the big red book, the lace and the scroll, will tell you *a story from long ago. We are all family,"* and with that said Cordren flew off to catch up with her family. She didn't want her parents to know she cared for Amy!

"Come on girl," Thunderbolt was shouting back at his daughter.

"What?" Amy screamed after Cordren. "That can't be right. Never, never! we cannot be related! And where has the book flown to?"

Amy thought she would have to ask her parents and her Aunt Flora to explain when she returned to Scotland. There would be so much for Amy to learn from the two sisters.

Katie the mermaid and the golden fairy lady, two more unusual girls and all of Cordren's family were related! How can that be? Amy was asking herself all these questions.

Chapter Fourteen
The Disappearing Castle and its Tower

Katie transported Amy and Jessica to the castle with a click of her magic camera. The castle was whole once more and in full view now.

"Over here," Robin called out to Amy who was still wondering why the castle kept disappearing.

Robin and his friends sat just outside the drawbridge where the portcullis was down blocking their way in. The guards were asking what their business was and hadn't taken notice as to who they were.

The fairy lady appeared and hovered close by the group of boys but out of view of the guards as they discussed the problem of should they let the boys in.

Jessica came up with a plan.

"You boys move close to the gate and we will go around the other side of the castle to find a different way in and then open this gate and let you in."

"Just keep the guards talking," Amy added.

"How are girls going to do that?" Robin turned to Little John, as the rest of the boys sniggered, as though girls were useless.

"You just wait," Jessica told them as she nodded to her girlfriends to follow her.

She knew Katie with the help of the camera would manage some magic. Amy could guess that Katie didn't want the boys to see her use her camera tucked away in its brown leather box and hung about Katie's neck.

Quickly making their way around the walls of the castle the girls came to stop before a wooden flagpole where a rope was dangling from a flapping flag of a red cross on a white background, the flag of England and the design on the cloth covering King Richard's chest of armour. This flag was named St Georges flag, after George killing the dragon. Amy remembered her history as she looked up at the tall wooden pole, least ways we never had to fight a dragon in this adventure! And Amy smiled to herself, was that another legend?

Katie stood with her camera focused on the rope, she told the girls to grab hold and as they held on Katie clicked a button and so all the girls began to slide slowly up the rope to land on a walkway spreading around the castles inner walls. From here they could run around to where the portcullis was closed and then jump down behind the guards to take them by surprise. Robin could point his arrows at the guards and take them prisoner, making them open the portcullis and that's just what happened.

Thomas thought that was great fun until he turned to see Prince John holding Marion by the little remaining hair on her head, the only part of her body anyone could see now. It was almost as though she had had her head chopped off and the Prince held it up as a trophy.

"We have to save her," Robin shouted out.

"Come on," Tom said as he waved his clenched fist at the Prince. He was ready for a fight!

More guards came dashing from inside the castle to stand by Prince John's side, their swords were drawn and ready to slice the boys dead!

The boys huddled themselves together in front of Katie who was trying to take aim with her camera. She would have to use it now and the boys would ask about its magic and she didn't want that. Just as she thought all was lost, galloping horses came charging over the drawbridge. Their hooves made such a din you would think a whole army had arrived when in fact it was only a few men led by King Richard.

All but Prince John knelt and bowed before the King.

"Arise," the king demanded, along with a wave of his hand.

Everyone stood but said nothing, just admiring this man who sat on a white stallion looking very regal and in charge.

Prince John was the first to speak, he wanted to tell his story, always trying to look the innocent person. Poor Marion had been dropped to the ground and now all that could be seen was a little head which laid on the grass a little way off from the crowd. Katie had seen Marion fall and had slipped away from the crowd to stand close by her. Looking down at Marion she asked how she could save her.

"The crow, the old witch, she sucked out my good inner self and I have been drifting away ever since. It is kept in that tower in a silver urn." And Marion moved her eyes towards the tower.

Katie needed to get inside that tower and while the rest of the people talked with the King she had her chance to walk away. It would not be easy to get inside because Katie knew the crow and the golden bird had both flown into the tower, what she didn't know was who the two were fighting.

But Katie would try to enter the tower and reach the urn and after all, she did have her trusted camera to help her.

It didn't take Katie long to find a ladder of stones moving up and close around the tower. Katie carefully climbed as there was no rail to hold as she moved around the wall.

Inside the tower, Katie watched as the witch and the fairy fought. One held a broomstick the other a magical twig with golden feathers attached to its end. Katie took her camera to focus on the two, what was she to do?

The old grandmother witch sensed Katie behind her and quickly swung around, her cloak making a swishing sound and a draft of air made the fairy fall to her side. At that point, Katie had just enough time to click the camera now focused on the fairy to transport her to the ground outside. Now for the witch, who held that silver urn, holding Marion's inner self in her hand. Katie must have it and so once again she used her camera. Finding the correct button on the camera's side she clicked at the urn which gently began to warm up, a pink glow turned to a red hot glow. Hotter and hotter the metal became until the old witch could no longer hold it. Her grey wrinkled hands burnt, she let go. Katie rushed forward and caught the cooling urn in her hand and dashed outside, the witch chasing behind her and her camera. Another button had been clicked and fast to save Katie from a spell.

As Katie reached the ground she turned to see the witch almost on top of her while sitting on her broomstick. Katie clicked a button and in an instant, the broomstick did a double sommersault and the witch fell to the ground where the mother fairy was waiting with her magic twig and with a flick of her wrist the witch disappeared, but where to? The fairy wouldn't say.

Katie sat on the grass close to Marion's head and massaged where she thought Marion's chest was, she opened the lid on the top of the urn, from where a pink curl of smoke floated over to Marion. Katie could feel a warmth coming from an invisible body which was slowly becoming visible. Marion began to take shape, her body reforming, filling out and soon she was whole again.

*

Jessica stood by, watching all of this and Robin running towards the forest; she turned and asked Marion why she wasn't going too.

"I will wait until Robin sees me as a young lady."

And no more was said as that was the right thing to do.

"We need to get back to our time," Amy said to Katie.

"But Amy you still don't have the book or the words," Jessica stated the obvious.

"I know but there must be a reason for that," she said in a disappointed voice.

*

King Richard was leading Prince John into the castle as Robin and his friends left by the drawbridge. There had been no huge fight after all. The grandmother witch had disappeared after the mother fairy had become a golden bird once again and had now flown off, but where were the words the bird had collected from the big red book?

Chapter Fifteen
The Cube Contains a Secret

Robin arrived back to his forest of Sherwood to lead his life, whatever that may be!

Katie had turned her camera towards the girls and Thomas ready to use the flash bulb and return them to their time. Thomas looked on in total disbelief.

Marion was whole again and safe with King Richard, who had taken her into his world, to be her guardian.

The fairy looked down from the trees and was pleased with the outcome, for she knew she would see the girls again, later, in their time.

She had known it was only Amy who could bring Jessica to Robin's time to make all of that happen, by her contact with Marion, as she had in this adventure.

Jessica was really the one that had saved Marion, as in her family history both girls were related and that's why they looked so very much alike. But of course, neither girl knew that; but they might just find out one day!

Good deeds to others always return good things in life to them who don't expect it, the fairy knew that and Jessica had been kind to Marion.

Just as Katie was about to click the button Amy called out,

"Stop! Where is the golden bird with the curly letters, my family secrets? I need them."

"You will find them safely locked away inside the Cube!" The sweet voice of the golden fairy floated down.

"What? But how will I read them? And, the big red book?" Amy shouted after the golden fairy lady whose voice faded away with her.

"Come back," Amy cried out.

But she was gone.

*

"I need to swim," Katie said and stretched her legs which had become very dry and itchy. "I must go, I will see you soon in Scotland, at a loch," and with that Katie ran off to find the river.

"When? Which loch?" Amy called after her, but Katie was gone.

Katie had clicked the camera, a white flash had come and gone. The time traveling flash gun on the top of her camera had transported them back to the lawn where all their school friends sat having a lecture from Mr Woodstock.

The three could hear other youngsters' voices chattering just off in the distance, voices that sounded familiar. They were back!

With a whoosh, Thomas and the girls found themselves standing at the back of their class who were sitting on the lawn.

"Sit down," Mr Woodstock demanded of the girls and Thomas who looked dazed as he sat. It was as though Mr Woodstock didn't even know they hadn't been there all the time.

As the girls looked around Amy felt cheated, where was the book with her story?

The castle had disappeared again and Marion was well back in her own time. Amy wouldn't be seeing her walk that lawn again.

As the lesson on the lawn finished Amy and Jessica headed inside the building and up to their room to change for dinner.

First, though Amy had to take out her cube from her bag of clothes placed under the bunk beds, to look inside. Holding the cube she was searching for an opening, a button, a hook anything, there was nothing, not even a handle, only one picture, that of a golden bird.

Looking at it in surprise she called Jessica over to look too. Amy touched the bird, it felt warm and as she touched it a sheet of paper fluttered from its beak. The paper was getting larger all the time before it landed beside Amy and to her amazement, there was a picture and writing to be read.

"My story."

A clue for Amy to follow.

Family Tree

U and Y

Family Flee

Y
Gold and Silver

Green and Black

U

Will be back

"Whatever could this mean?"

Amy covered her mouth after she had spoken the words out loud.

"Let's think over dinner," Jessica took up the puzzle in her mind.

Going down for dinner that last evening of the trip to Nottingham, Jessica asked a few of their class friends if anyone had seen Tom. Most hadn't but Sam had.

"Oh, Mr Woodstock was chasing after him for being late the other day after shooting the arrows into a tree instead of the target!"

"Really? So where is he now?" No one seemed to know.

After their meal, the two girls decided to go outside and look for Thomas. After a while of wandering the grounds, they went to the museum building which was open late that evening, for the last of the project work to be completed by Mr Woodstock. Amy was the first to see him in the art room studying the paintings.

"Here you are, I have been searching for you."

Amy could see Thomas looked worried.

"What's up?" Jessica appeared behind Amy and asked the question.

"Nothing," Thomas said.

He was trying to understand where he had been, who those people were in the paintings.

"Come on Tom, Amy took his arm and the three walked back to their dormitories for a night's sleep before the long journey home to Scotland the next day.

One painting shone out a golden light from an old Oak tree where a boy stood underneath waving his hand but Amy never noticed.

I hope you enjoy these stories, look out for the next ones when Amy becomes a teenager and uses the Cube the Golden Fairy Lady gave to her.

Read how she works her way through understanding her family and how to use her new found powers. Read about Jessica and Thomas and how they fit into Amy's adventures.

All my books are available at Amazon as paperbacks or on kindle.

Thank-you for buying my books and happy reading.

from Jasmine.

www.jasmine-appleton.co.uk